TO WENDY—who knows it takes more than words
and pictures to make a book
and
TO NONNY—who knows what makes a great cake

Book design by Kristen M. Nobles.
Typeset in Circus Mouse Book and Vag Rounded.
The illustrations for this book were rendered in Caran D'ache oil pastels on black Canson paper.
Manufactured in Hong Kong.

Library of Congress Cataloging-in-Publication Data
Coffelt, Nancy.
What's cookin'? : a happy birthday counting book / by Nancy Coffelt.
p. cm.
Summary: One by one, ten cooks arrive to help bake a great big birthday surprise.
ISBN 0-8118-3561-8
[1. Baking-Fiction. 2. Cakes—Fiction. 3. Birthdays—Fiction.
4. Counting.] I. Title.
PZ7.C658 Wh 2003
[E]—dc21
2002003517

Distributed in Canada by Raincoast Books
9050 Shaughnessy Street, Vancouver, British Columbia V6P 6E5

10 9 8 7 6 5 4 3 2 1

Chronicle Books LLC
85 Second Street, San Francisco, California 94105

www.chroniclekids.com

What's Cookin'?

A Happy Birthday Counting Book

by Nancy Coffelt

chronicle books · san francisco

In the kitchen,
the sunny kitchen,
the clock tick-tocks,
the faucet drip-drops,
the refrigerator hums,

and the cook grabs a spoon.

A second cook soon ambles in.

Knock
Knock

"I'm here to help you.
Let's begin!"

Knock

Knock

Knock

Stand aside—cook coming through!
Cook Number Three has work to do.

"I'm here to
sift the flour."

3

Knock

Knock

Knock

Knock

Another cook is at the door.
One, Two, Three—and now here's Four.

"I'm here to measure the sugar."

4

The kitchen's buzzing like a hive.
Four cooks make room for Number Five.

"I'm here to crack the eggs."

Knock

Knock

Knock

Knock

Knock

Knock

Knock

Knock

Knock

Knock

Knock

Here's Number Six.

"I'm here to mix."

The next one in will have to squeeze—
make room for Number Seven, please.

"I'm here to
pour the batter."

7

Cook Number Eight, arriving late,

is just in time
to bake the cake.

Knock
Knock
Knock
Knock
Knock
Knock
Knock
Knock
Knock

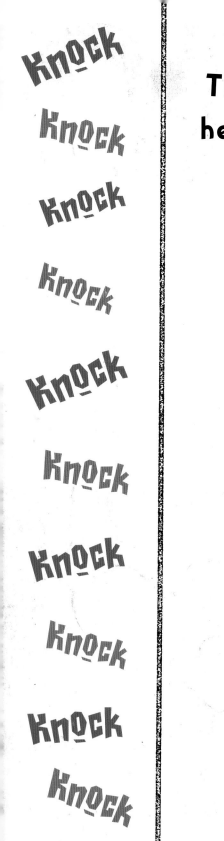

The door flies open once again—
here come Numbers Nine and Ten.

"This place is
such an awful mess.

9

We'll help you clean it up, I guess."

10

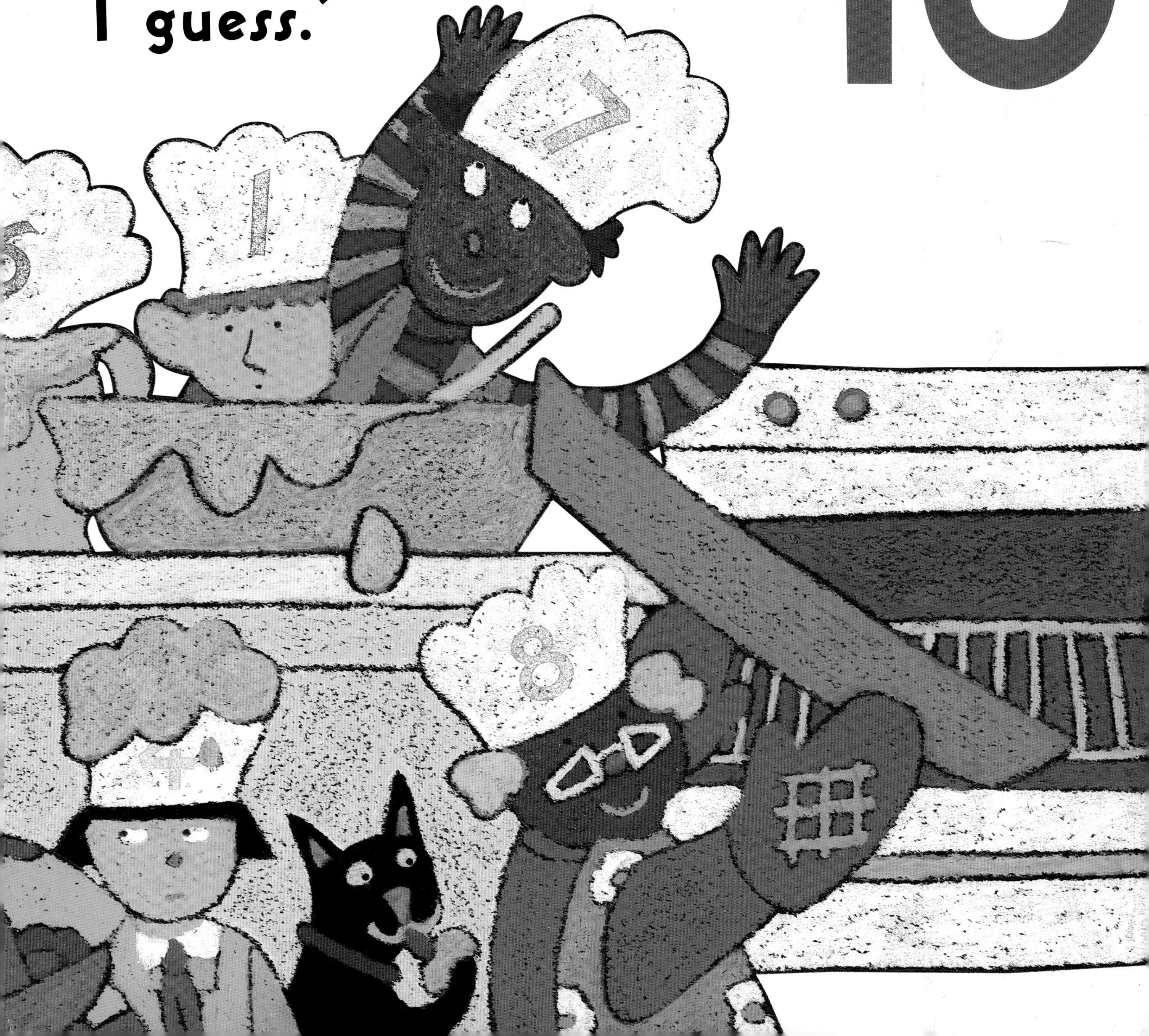

Ten grabs the bucket.
Nine grabs the mop.
Eight clears the dishes
off the countertop.

Seven takes the cake out.
Six cleans spoons.
Five makes the frosting.
Four blows balloons.

Three brings out the candles.

"Light them up!" Two cries.

Says Number One,

"This cake is done!"

They all yell,

Tips for Cooking with a Child

Young children love to help in the kitchen, especially when the result is cookies or cake. Here are some suggestions for making cooking with your child a rewarding experience.

- Keep it simple. Baking a cake from scratch is fun, and your child may enjoy doing it the "old-fashioned" way. But cake mixes are an easy substitute and close to foolproof.

- Be prepared. Gather all your equipment and ingredients before you start. This allows you to give your full attention to the child.

- Keep careful watch. Keep sharp knives and mixer blades out of the child's reach, and make sure the child understands that using electrical appliances, the stovetop, and the oven is your job.

Math in the Kitchen

The kitchen is a perfect laboratory for teaching early math skills. Here are some simple, fun math activities.

- Fill a measuring cup with chocolate chips or raisins. Ask the child to guess how many are in the cup. You guess too. Then spill the contents onto the counter or tabletop and count them with the child.

- Help the child divide them into groups of fives or tens.

- Fill the measuring cup again, this time with miniature marshmallows or olives. Are there more or fewer in the cup? Why?

- Pour half a cup of water into a tall, skinny glass and half a cup of water into a short, fat glass. Ask the child to guess which glass holds more water. Because the water will be higher in the tall glass, the child will probably guess that one. Now pour the water from each glass into the measuring cup. Your child will be surprised to see there is the same amount of water in each glass.

Cousin Alice's
Easy Layer Cake

Ingredients

½ cup soft margarine or shortening
1½ cups sugar
1 cup milk
2¼ cups cake flour
1 teaspoon salt
2 teaspoons baking powder
2 teaspoons vanilla extract
3 eggs

You will need

Large mixing bowl
Electric mixer
Measuring cups
Measuring spoons
Wooden spoon or spatula
    for scraping the bowl
2 round baking pans (8 inches)

Directions

1. Preheat the oven to 350°F.

2. Prepare the cake pans by greasing them lightly with margarine, shortening, or vegetable oil, then sprinkling them with flour. Shake the pans to distribute the flour evenly, then discard the excess flour.

3. Mix the margarine or shortening and the sugar until blended. The batter will be crumbly.

4. Add the milk and continue mixing. The batter will now be wet and crumbly.

5. Add the flour and mix until blended.

6. Add the salt, baking powder, vanilla, and eggs. Mix until blended.

7. Pour the batter into the cake pans and place them on the middle rack of the oven.

8. Bake for 35 minutes.

9. Cool the cakes in the pans for 10 minutes, then remove them from the pans and frost.

Quick Chocolate Frosting

1 can (14 ounces) of sweetened condensed milk
1 cup chocolate chips

Heat the milk and chocolate chips over low heat, stirring until completely blended. Cool before frosting.

Quick Cream Cheese Frosting

3 ounces softened cream cheese
3/4 cup sifted powdered sugar
1 1/2 tablespoons milk
1 teaspoon vanilla

Mix all the ingredients until smooth and creamy.

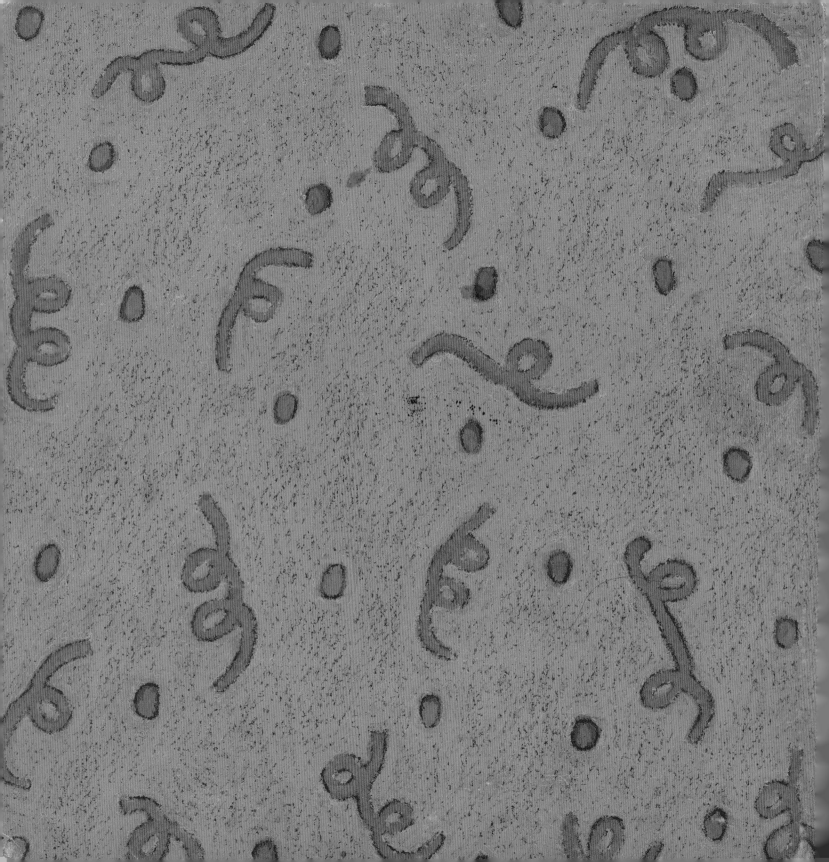